THIS BOOK BELONGS TO:

_____

_____

_____

Find me on each picture

PETE

PARASAUROPHUS

PTEROSAUR

TERRY

REX

THE TYRANNOSAURUS REX

IGUANODON

IGGY

VELACIRAPTOR

VICTOR

SPINOSAURUS

SHELLY

Agnes Green
Visit my website at www.apriltalebooks.com

Printed in the United States of America
First Printing: August 2019

www.apriltalebooks.com

10 DINOSAURS PARTY TIME

Author
AGNES GREEN

Illustrator
ZHANNA MENDEL

It's dinosaur party time! All the guests are there,
With big balloons and ribbons and fun hats to wear.

It's just getting started – it's only just begun.
Maybe if we're lucky, we can join in all the fun!

Ten little dinosaurs are dancing on the floor.
They shake their tails and stomp around, then do it all the more!

Trixie the Triceratops starts a conga line,
But Rex's arms are just too short and he soon falls behind.

Nine little dinosaurs are playing musical bumps...
Every time the music stops, they sit down with a thump!

The raptors' quick; he always gets whichever chair is near,
But this time when the others sit, he seems to disappear.

Eight little dinosaurs take turns to bounce up high.
They're all so heavy; when they jump, they almost touch the sky,

It's Steggy's turn to have a jump and join in with the gang,
But when his spiky tail comes down, he pops it with a BANG.

Seven little dinosaurs are running in a race.
They all want to win it – there's a trophy for first place.

Spinosaurus finds a shortcut and so takes a sneaky ride,
But Daddysaurus spots her and she gets disqualified.

Six little dinosaurs are playing hide and seek.
Now you have to understand, this is not an easy feat.

It's hard to hide your body when it's quite so long and tall...
Dippy stomps away and sulks: *"I cannot play this game at all!"*

Five little dinosaurs are choosing fancy dress.
They've got fairy wands and pirate hats and capes and all the rest,

Trixie wants to be the world's first ballet-dancing dino.
Although, when she twirls off through the air, she looks more like a rhino.

Four little dinosaurs are singing very loudly.
Pete's the loudest of them all – he toots his horn quite proudly.

He's drowning out the singing saurs and making such a din,
That when he turns the other way, they run away from him.

Three little dinosaurs are gathered round the cake—
But not just any cake, because it's really made of steak.

The dinos blow the candles out and shout three cheers: *"Hooray!"*
But look, they puffed so hard they've blown poor pterosaur away.

Two little dinosaurs want a bite to eat;
One munches up the plants, the other one eats meat.

Allan Allosaurus swallows down the whole steak cake:
It was much too big and now he's got an awful tummy ache.

One little dinosaur is turning out the light;
He's partied out and sleepy so it's time to say goodnight.

We've had a ROAR, it's been a BLAST, but now we need a rest...
Prehistoric dino parties really are the best.

Thanks for stomping by!

Thank you for reading!
I hope you enjoyed
this cute little story!

Reviews from awesome customers
like you help others to feel confident
about choosing this book too.

Please take a minute to review it
and share your experience!

Thank you in advance
for helping me out!
I will be forever grateful.

Yours, Agnes Green

"It's time for bed... Hip hip hooray! Let's all give a cheer!
The day is through. We've had such fun. Now sleepy time draws near.

Before you drift away to dream, let's check in at the zoo.
I hear they're having a parade and a pajama party too!"

Don't miss another book of mine!
"Today I'm a Monster"

Made in the USA
Coppell, TX
24 November 2019

11843679R00024